Black Tears

Black Tears

Gerd Darner

VANTAGE PRESS
New York

To the Society for the Prevention of Cruelty to
Animals (SPCA)

Black Tears

CHAPTER

ONE

The sun—orange in color in a grey-blue April sky—was setting over Frogner Park. The park was just waking up after a long and cold winter, the grass was brownish and wet, and the soil smelt fresh and sweet. The river was playing gaily under the bridge and sent cascades of water over the crocuses already in flower amongst the rocks. There were not many people in the park, and the air was brisk, cold, and clear.

A large red ball was thrown high up in the air and landed on the riverside amongst the rocks, but it was not there for long. An athletic red boxer dog caught the ball quick as lightning and ran happily with it back to his owner and placed it at her feet. He looked at her with warm, black, and large eyes as though to say, "Throw the ball again!"

This time the ball landed in the river. In a flash the dog was there again, and the ball was placed in front of the woman's feet. The boxer looked at her with a trusting look. "Throw the ball again, p-l-e-a-s-e."

The young, handsome girl took the ball under her arm and looked towards the setting sun. The sky was now in flames, the sun's rays colouring the park, the girl, and the dog.

They went home slowly. As usual, both of them had plenty of time, and the house was not far away. The girl's father was working in the garden, and the dog wagged his tail in joy. Again the red ball was thrown amongst the bushes and an eager boxer caught it immediately.

Then all three entered the white house, and the young woman put the ball on the shelf above the fireplace. The home was old and beautifully furnished with art and antiques, all collected by Dr. Berg himself. Now he called to the girl, Laila, and said, "Fetch a bottle of wine in the cellar, and we shall have a cosy hour in front of the fire. It is rather chilly tonight, and we shall celebrate the new job you are starting tomorrow."

Laila ran down the stairs, as always closely followed by Pan. She had had to discontinue her medical studies at the university temporarily due to a number of disturbances and difficulties there and would be starting as a secretary to the father of a girlfriend the following day.

They sat around the fireplace, the three of them, and Laila and her father talked about the future. It was mostly Dr. Berg who did the talking; he was insisting that Laila continue her studies after the war. She had to promise him this.

He sat still, looking at Laila. His own little Laila was a true copy of the doctor's deceased wife, with light blonde hair and blue eyes, slim and well built. He also admired her dog, Pan, with his shiny red coat, black face, and big black eyes, which shone in devotion to his mistress. The doctor was glad that Laila had this true friend in these difficult times.

He went over to the grand piano and played from Bach, his favourite composer. They were both silent as the music, soft and pleasant, filled the room.

"Now I want to go to bed," he said suddenly. "I have several operations tomorrow, so good night, both of you, and sleep well." He waved his hand. Laila smiled, and Pan wagged his tail.

Finally, they too also went to bed. It was cold for April. It was night, night over Oslo town.

Next day came with rain and fog. Dr. Berg was an early riser, and as usual he walked the long way to the hospital. Somewhat later Laila had her breakfast served in the kitchen by kind old Anne. Anne, who had been with the family since Laila was born, looked after the two well, Laila and the dog. Anne complained as usual about the Germans, the rationing, and her rheumatism.

"So long, Pan," Laila smiled and patted the dog. "I will be back just after four o'clock." All of a sudden Laila pressed the dog closely to her and kissed him between the eyes; then she ran through the door, slamming it.

"That poor old dog," Anne said.

Pan went to his usual place and the red ball. He was completely relaxed, waiting for his mistress and big love to come back.

It was eleven o'clock when the bell rang and Anne opened the door. She got a fright when she saw a officer from the Gestapo and two civilians. Her face turned white as chalk as she thought of Laila and whether they had arrested her.

They wanted to come inside, but Anne would not let them. They pushed farther into the room and followed her. Pan was snarling and snapping at them, but a big, begloved Gestapo hand tightened a chain around his neck and shouted in broken Norwegian, "We are taking this dog with us! Here are the necessary papers and documents!"

Anne was terrified, and she was wailing all the time. "Do not take Laila's dog. Give me back the dog." She tried hopelessly to grab Pan, but he was dragged through the door and out to a waiting car.

Anne went over to the telephone and phoned the hospital. It took quite some time before she got through to the surgery. A nurse said, "It is for you, Dr. Berg."

He got very annoyed. "I don't take

phone calls here in the surgery; you should know that."

"It is very important," the nurse said again.

Dr. Berg took the phone and listened. After a while they could see his hand trembling and all colour leaving his face. They had never seen him like that before, this fabulous brain surgeon known all over the Western world.

He put the receiver back and, turning to his colleague, said, in a low voice, "Lund, you have to take over; I have to go."

He tried to get a taxi, but there were none in sight. He ran across the street to the bus stop and jumped on the first bus going to the centre of town. He arrived finally at Gestapo headquarters and gave his card to the guard outside. He was escorted into an office, and a German officer smiled at him and tried to shake his hand. "What can I do for the famous surgeon?" he asked.

9

Cato Berg looked coldly at him and said in a husky voice, "Let me have my dog, Pan, back." He banged his fist on the desk in front of him.

"Oh, is that all, a dog gone astray?" The officer sat down and lit a cigarette, offering one to the doctor, but the doctor did not even notice it. "A dog," repeated the officer.

He took the telephone and, turning to the doctor, said, "I shall check up on this."

He took several phone calls and finally gave his report. "All the dogs requisitioned are now aboard a plane en route for Germany. There is nothing I or anybody else can do in this matter. But, my God, it is only a dog, and you shall receive compensation." He looked at the Norwegian standing in front of him. "After all, it is not a human being."

The doctor, with intense hate showing all over his face, making the officer fall back, said with a trembling voice, "No, it is much more, very much more."

It was a happy Laila leaving the bus in the afternoon and running home. It had stopped raining, and her blonde hair was waving in the wind.

"Pan!" she called out as she entered the hall. "Pan, my boy, where are you? Don't fool around!"

She was met by two serious and sad faces. She fell back and cried, "He is not dead, is he? Answer me!"

Her father said: "Listen, Laila dear. Sit down. The Germans have requisitioned Pan and sent him to Germany, but surely we shall have him back again."

Anne was crying all the time, and Laila's father had broken down. Laila ran up to her room, locking the door.

There was nothing the two old people could do. They were completely lost, angry and helpless and full of sorrow.

Their thoughts went to the beautiful dog with the black eyes—Laila's great love. How frightened he must be now, and how he must miss them all.

CHAPTER

TWO

Germany, 1943

On arrival at the airport in Germany, the dogs were loaded on large trucks. One dog tried to escape but was quickly caught. Pan had also thought of trying to get away but changed his mind.

All the dogs were barking all the time. *What is the use?* Pan said to himself and found himself a place in a corner where he was more comfortable and where he saw a small boxer who was obviously very frightened.

Poor little thing, thought Pan as the little boxer pressed herself against Pan, trembling all over. Pan was also frightened but did not like to show it. The trip on the plane had been even more frightening. Now Pan was angrier and wondered what was going to happen. *Where is Laila? Where is my red ball? Where is my house?*

It was a long drive, but finally the truck stopped and the dogs were taken into a large hall with a number of separate enclosures. Pan and the small boxer were lucky, as they were sharing the same compartment. They were given some food and water, but most of the dogs did not touch it. Pan was hungry and took the food given to him, but the small boxer did not touch anything, not even water.

All of a sudden the hall was lit up by several searchlights and a number of people came around to inspect the dogs. They were all measured and each got a new collar stamped *Wehrmacht* and with his name and a number. *Now they will send me back,* said Pan to himself, but instead the lights went off and it was dark.

Pan could not sleep. He thought of Laila and could not stop the sorrow.

It had been a long and strenuous day, but finally Pan went off to sleep, to be awakened by a number of soldiers, each collecting one dog. Pan was picked out by a young, fair boy. He looked nice and kind, and Pan followed him without any protests. On a large exercise court all the dogs were assembled, and Pan also noticed his small boxer friend was amongst them.

A man about thirty years of age entered the ring with one boxer on each side. He was rather small but athletic-looking, with brown eyes, moustache, and a healthy tan. He surveyed the dogs and the men, wishing them welcome to the Wehrmacht's training camp.

"You are here to fight for your country," he said. "Most of you will be attached to the Medical Corps to pick up

17

dead and wounded on the field. It is your duty to look after the dogs, respect them, and treat them properly. The dogs are needed at the front, where they play an important part."

Kurt Zimmermann went around and inspected each dog, patting some of them on the head and saying a few kind words. Then he went back into the ring and with his large boxer demonstrated what the training was all about. Finally he harnessed his boxer to a sledge and showed how they should cross a battlefield, lying low and eluding the dangers. Pan was fascinated by this exhibition and looked forward to trying it himself.

The training started again, and when finally Pan was led back to the large hall he was all worn out and fell asleep immediately. He woke up when he heard the voice of Kurt Zimmermann talking to the small boxer next to him.

"Poor little Bambi," Zimmermann

said, patting her on the head. "You are the most beautiful dog I have ever seen, but you are very small."

Then he discovered Pan watching him and listening to him. Pan tried to come closer, but the chain kept him back, so Zimmermann went across to him and inspected his collar. "Pan," he said. "Pan from Norway. A god."

"You are big and husky," he continued, smiling at Pan, "a real army dog." He patted Pan and the dog felt a sort of happiness as he looked at Zimmermann with pleading eyes as if to say, "Send me back; send me home to Laila."

Pan only kept company with the small, beautiful Bambi, who followed him like a shadow. Pan was sure of himself and was Bambi's only comfort. They appeared to be happy being together most of the day, but they were both missing their people terribly. On the training ground Pan tried his ut-

19

most to succeed and be patted and rewarded by Kurt Zimmermann. He missed someone to love.

The training went on for weeks. The dogs had now practically finished their training, and Pan was the best of the lot. Kurt Zimmermann was obviously pleased with him, although Kurt's great love was Bambi.

"Do you want to leave and come with me?" asked Kurt Zimmermann, looking at Pan. They both jumped into an old car and drove towards Berlin. Pan had not seen a large town for a long time, and his thoughts went back to Oslo. After an hour the car stopped outside a large, dreary-looking building. They were met by a small, dark woman and a little boy.

"Daddy!" cried the boy, happily greeting his father, and then he hugged Pan like Laila had done in the old days. And when the boy got a large ball to play with, Pan forgot everything and they played together for several hours. Pan was in ecstasy and when finally the boy had to go to bed Pan was allowed to sleep at the foot of the bed. He was in seventh heaven, and when the boy went to sleep he crept carefully up to the boy and rested quietly next to him. This was just what Pan was used to when he stayed with Laila, and watching the little boy with his large black eyes, Pan's sorrow shone from his large eyes. Pan did not notice that there was someone else in the room.

"Poor dog," said Mrs. Zimmermann, "poor dog."

"He comes from Norway, and his name is Pan," said Kurt Zimmermann.

"Fancy giving one's dog to the Wehrmacht, or is it to the führer?" She smiled contemptuously.

"Yes, such is war," answered Kurt. He did not reveal his real thoughts. "Pan," he said, shaking him by the coat,

"Pan, the leave is over, my friend. We have to be off."

He kissed his little sleeping boy good night and hugged his wife, and he and Pan were off.

Kurt Zimmermann had a special hand with the dogs. He was strict, but in the right way. They all respected him and obeyed him.

Poor little Bambi had great difficulties with the sledges. She was willing and tried hard, but every time she was put to the sledges she got desperate and ran along faster than anybody else in the camp. She was as elegant as an antelope, and Kurt Zimmermann did not give in. He trained and trained Bambi, and finally he was more or less satisfied she could do the job required.

The camp was like all camps, dreary and grey, all fenced in. Every day the dogs had an hour off when they could play together, ambulance dogs and watchdogs. And quite a few times it ended in several fights. One Alsatian especially was notorious for his temperament. He picked a quarrel with everybody, mostly with a dog named Pluto, and they kept on fighting until someone managed to tear them apart. Pluto was the largest boxer in the camp, but of good nature and only picked a fight when he was bored. He only fought the watchdogs, though.

Pan and Bambi used to watch the fights from a safe distance, but this particular day the quarrelsome Alsatian did not feel like fighting Pluto and instead had picked out Bambi as a victim. Bambi had never been in a fight in her life, so she was terrified and ran along the fence. But the Alsatian cornered her easily and put his teeth right into her body. She was thrown up in the air, and the Alsatian kept on harassing her.

Pan was there like lightning. He saw

Bambi lying on the ground badly torn, and with a terrific jump he landed on top of the Alsatian, turned him around, and got his teeth in the dog's throat. He sat on his opponent's stomach and forced the wind out of him. Pan was really choking the brute when he saw dimly and half in fury an SS officer who trained the watchdogs come running towards him with a pistol in his hand. Pan knew he would be shot. He let the Alsatian go and instead attacked the SS officer, flattening him to the ground, and twisted the gun out of his hand, as Kurt Zimmermann had taught him. He sat on the officer, holding him to the ground, and could see Bambi lying a few yards away bleeding badly and a helpless Alsatian on his other side. Pan fought for his life, and he knew it. He had in mind to kill them both, the Alsatian and the SS officer, when Kurt Zimmermann appeared, dragging him away from the SS officer, a farm boy from Bayern named Wolfgang Stern.

"Give me my gun!" Wolfgang Stern shouted in fury. "I shall kill that bloody bastard! Look what he has done!" He was running around in circles out of his wits.

"Shut up!" Kurt Zimmermann called back at him. "Shut up and take that miserable beast with you."

Pan was sitting watching Bambi and could not believe what he saw.

"Take her to the surgery," Kurt Zimmermann commanded.

The fair young boy who normally looked after Bambi lifted her up and carried her in his arms. Pan trotted along after him.

The veterinary surgeon shook his head when he saw Bambi and said, "There is nothing I can do; we shall have to put her to sleep."

"You will do no such thing!" Kurt

25

Zimmermann cried out. "Save Bambi's life, if it is the last thing you ever do!"

His friend the doctor looked at him, then at Pan, saying, "Come here, you!"

"We shall have to try a blood transfusion."

He put some long needles into Pan's veins. Pan did not object; he just lay there feeling weaker and weaker as he watched how his blood disappeared into his dear Bambi. Finally they took the needles away, Bambi was given an injection, and the doctor started stitching her up. Pan rested under a chair, his eyes full of black tears.

"Look, he is crying over his friend; he is crying black tears," one of the soldiers said. They all looked at Pan in wonder; they had never seen a dog shed black tears, and they felt sort of funny.

All through the night Pan and Kurt Zimmermann were watching over dear little Bambi. She got a further blood transfusion; this time they used Pluto as donor.

The following morning Bambi woke up. She was in a terrible state. She had lost one eye. Across the neck was a big scar where part of her coat had been torn away. But the stomach was even worse, stitch upon stitch. Kurt Zimmermann gave her some water, and Pan kissed her gently on her forehead as Laila used to kiss him good night. He was so gentle, as he was afraid of hurting her.

Bambi's attendant, patting her carefully, all of a sudden started to cry. "We shall make it," he sobbed. "You just wait and see."

He left the room quietly whilst Kurt Zimmermann raged, cursing all and everybody. Finally he relaxed and sat down next to Bambi. He dragged Pan to him and held him tight, whispering, "Let us two remember Bambi as she was, truly the world's most beautiful boxer, with a beautiful face, and we both love her. I can tell you, Pan, I know what I am talking about, as I was brought up on a large estate breeding horses and boxers. Bambi was a real beauty, a revelation. But not a soldier, Pan, she was not a soldier. We must remember her as she was," he said sadly.

Pan placed his head in Kurt's lap, licking his hand. Then he lay down close to Bambi to show her how he loved her. He looked at Kurt Zimmermann, his friend, and wagged his tail as if saying, "Thank you, my dear friend; thank you for saving her."

Kurt Zimmermann smiled, left the room and loudly said, mostly to himself, "You must be a hell of a man."

Days and weeks passed with the same routine. Pan was, as before, eager to learn and never left Bambi. He knew that in Bambi he had a friend for life;

on the other hand he also had an enemy, Wolfgang Stern, who was always after him, and Pan did his best to avoid him. A hate had grown between these two of a type that occurs very seldom between man and dog. Kurt Zimmermann was aware of this and tried to calm Pan down. He spent much too much time with Pan and Bambi, and he knew it, but there was nothing he could do about it. He admired these two Norwegian boxers, Pan, big and strong, and Bambi, small and always frightened. He always saw Bambi as she was before the accident, with perfect head and shining eyes. He even dreamt about her at night.

One morning they were called earlier than usual and transported on large trucks to a large training camp in a forest. Pan saw Bambi being taken away by an officer for training, and all of a sudden Wolfgang Stern was at his side. Pan was tied up to a tree trunk, and Stern started slashing him with a riding whip. There were gunshots all around him as part of the training, and Pan's loud cries of pain were drowned out by the cannonade. Wolfgang Stern then went on kicking Pan with his heavy boots, once in the eye, but mostly in the stomach. Pan was in terrible pain, and he nearly passed out from loss of blood. He cried out in all force, dragging at the lead that nearly choked him, and all of a sudden the lead gave way and he was free. He ran towards the others with the SS officer chasing him, shooting wildly at him.

Then suddenly Wolfgang Stern felt an iron arm grabbing him by the coat and turning him around, and he was face to face with the commandant.

"What in hell is this?" he shouted. "We don't shoot dogs. Speak up." He held Stern in a tighter grip.

Kurt Zimmermann was also there now and looked at Pan in awe.

"I must shoot that bastard!" shouted Stern. "He is a man hater."

"Far from it," said Zimmermann, "he is the best dog in the whole unit." He lifted Pan carefully and carried him off.

Stern left them with a cruel smile.

"Is he alive?"

"What has happened?"

A crowd had assembled around Kurt Zimmermann, who together with a doctor was trying to clean up all the blood so the doctor could examine Pan.

"Apart from what we can see of damage, he must have got internal bleeding, and we have to treat him very carefully. Let us hope he will pull through," the doctor said softly.

Kurt Zimmermann carried Pan to his car and placed him in the backseat and called little Bambi.

For many days Pan was on the danger list, but he made it. He woke up with Bambi at his side, Bambi, his love. But his hate for Stern had grown, a hate that would last forever.

CHAPTER

THREE

The eastern front

Then came the great day, the last day in the training camp. It was a grey autumn day with sleet and rain. Bambi felt very cold and sat close to her friend, and Pan was also shivering. At last Kurt Zimmermann arrived. As usual, he stood in the middle of the ring, gazing at the men and the dogs. He cleared his throat and spoke to them.

"Tomorrow, my friends, you will be at the front, you with boxers with the Medical Corps and the rest of you with dogs keeping watch. You are all trained to fight as soldiers for the *Vaterland*. Some of you men will return; some will be decorated and called heroes. But

35

some of you will never come back. Your dogs always die out there; they will not return and they will not receive any decorations and be called heroes. They will all be forgotten, but for the men here and the soldiers they save. They will never forget the dogs. It is their job to save as many lives as possible, at the expense of their own lives."

Kurt Zimmermann clicked his heels, turned abruptly around, and left them.

They were all called up and placed on the large trucks that had arrived. Pan found his Bambi and kept close to her. He tried to lift the tarpaulin in order to get a glimpse of Kurt Zimmermann, but the tarpaulin was too heavy. Suddenly he felt very lonely in the dark and was near crying. Instead he kissed Bambi's head, as if saying, "Don't be frightened. I am here with you."

They had a long wait at the airport, and it was bitterly cold. Finally they were all on board the plane and had received some food and water. The big engines made a frightening noise, and then they were off.

Pan had experienced this before at Oslo Airport, and he felt uncomfortable and frightened. The dogs eventually fell asleep and did not awake until the plane hit the ground, which was rather bumpy and covered with snow.

After a while the heavy door opened and the dogs were taken out, one by one. Pan saw Bambi led out and tried in vain to get loose from his chain, as he was afraid of being separated from Bambi. He started barking and at last someone came and took him out and Pan saw a white, cold landscape with some cars disappearing in a northern direction. But no Bambi.

"We will take him in the jeep," one officer said, and two officers placed themselves in the front seat and they were off on the icy road. Pan was more or less paralysed at the thought of losing Bambi and started whimpering feeling very sorry for himself.

"So you are the champion this time. I hope you fare better than the other two before you," the elder one said, a rather fat, small man with a round reddish face. He patted Pan on the head.

The driver was thin, tall, and nearly bald, although his face was young. "Yes, let us hope you have more luck. But you look very cold." He smiled at Pan. "Come and sit in front here; it is much warmer here."

Pan wagged his tail and licked the thin man's neck and jumped up between the two in the front seat. He felt like a grown soldier and liked it.

A group of houses appeared in the far distance, and Pan understood that this was their destination. Coming nearer, he saw the Red Cross banner and several tents placed in a group. The jeep stopped in front of a large tent, and

Pan was taken inside. There was a large stove in a corner and a writing desk, and two officers were sitting at a table, smoking. The man behind the desk arose, and the soldiers left, saluting.

Pan sat down and his black eyes were staring right into the blue eyes of Baron Otto von Riedler. Pan looked at him with trust and wagged his tail when von Riedler took his outstretched paw in his hand. Pan knew this was to be his new master, and he liked what he saw. The baron was tall and athletic-looking, with an aristocratic face and long, sinewy fingers. When he talked to the men his voice was angry, and Pan wondered how a man with such mild and kind eyes could be so angry. Pan was watching him all the time, and finally the baron sat down.

"You must be a von Dom," the baron said to Pan. "Come here, Cook!" he shouted at a man standing outside, a thick, heavy man with a slight limp.

"Look at these cat paws. I wish my old man could see them. They are typical of dogs from the Von Dom kennel. And he always said his old boxer, Skipper, was the only dog with cat paws."

"It was a great pity that Skipper died," said the cook. "He was the finest boxer in this country."

"Oh, never mind Skipper," the baron said angrily, as he got up and walked towards Pan, watching him carefully. Pan looked back at him, and they looked just like two fighting cocks.

"Go and sit down," he said in a milder voice.

Pan went and lay down on a sofa with cushions that he had been admiring for some time, and it reminded him of Laila's bed. The baron, without changing a feature in his face, helped himself to some wine. On his desk was a photo of a large white house and an old man with a boxer at his side. Seeing this, Pan suddenly got up and went across to the baron, putting his head in the baron's lap.

The cook gave Pan a generous meal, and Pan, satisfied, jumped up on his sofa and dreamt about his Bambi.

The cook smiled, picked up Pan's tray, and hoped the baron would have this dog for a long time; it would help him feel less lonely. "What is his name?" he asked in a whisper.

"Pan," said the baron, "Pan, a god."

Baron von Riedler was about forty years of age, handsome, elegant, and sometimes rather arrogant. He was born and bred on a large estate, and the family also had a residence in Berlin. The baron was used to riches, art, horses, and dogs. He was also a recognised surgeon, a master in his field, and a bachelor. He was disliked by some and loved by others, particularly those whose lives he had saved. When you first arrived at his field hospital you had a fair chance of pulling through under his hands. He did not allow anybody to come close to him, although quite a few wanted to be his friend. He had always had a big mouth, and as the war went on his voice grew angrier and angrier. He had only one soft point: boxers. He was himself fully convinced that no one knew about his weakness, but the cook knew of it, although the baron was not aware of this.

Pan got friendly with most men in the camp. Some were convalescents soon to be sent back to the front. Others, walking on crutches, were waiting to be transported home. The baron's days were fully occupied, most of the time in the surgery. There was quite a number of doctors attached to the field hospital, and they all worked hard. The surgery was in an old house, badly isolated, and quite a few of the patients had their beds in large heated tents.

Pan had become very friendly with

the thin officer who had collected him at the airport. Fritz Müller was his name, and he enjoyed talking to Pan. Pan trotted around the whole camp and visited the field kitchen as often as he had a chance. The cook always had something to give him, and under his stove Pan could rest for hours, the place being nice and warm.

Pan also visited the wounded, and when somebody was dying the dog sat at their bedside, trying to comfort them in his way. When someone had died Pan went out on the stairs and looked up at the sky with sad black eyes and they all knew that another bed was vacant.

"You will never die, Pan; you have too many friends up there watching over you," the cook said to him one day. "Nobody has as many dead friends as you have," he added, giving Pan a bone. "Pan was a god, the baron told me," and Pan gave his paw, thanking him for the bone.

The days went on and it was cold and bitter. Then one day the baron said to Pan as he was leaving for the surgery, "Today you must be back in the tent early. It is Christmas Eve and we shall celebrate together with our last bottle of wine, understood?"

Pan nodded affirmingly and followed the baron on his way to the surgery.

All of a sudden the whole area was lit up by an explosion. Fires broke out at several places, and the field hospital was in flames. They heard people crying and shouting, and Pan was paralysed with fear. The smoke smarting his eyes, Pan saw the cook lying on the ground and run towards him. "Come here, Pan!" the baron called out. "Come back!" Pan did not know what to do, but the baron got hold of his chain and held him back.

The actual surgery was not damaged, but the rest of the hospital was all in flames and black smoke. Pan tried to get loose. He wanted to help the wounded, as he could hear their terrible cries. He also wanted to look for the cook. Someone tried to get the wounded out of the burning building, but the heat and the smoke were too intense and they had to give it up. Von Riedler gave his orders, and they could hear his angry voice all over the camp. Fritz had now taken over Pan, and together with two soldiers they went to the far end of the camp, scouting toward a clump of trees where they could see wounded solders who had been on the way to the hospital.

"What has happened?" one of the soldiers asked Fritz.

"Our men were pursued by partisans, and thus they found this hospital and blew up most of it before getting away. They are still in the forest, though."

"We must help the wounded and get

across to them. Cover us!" Fritz shouted to the soldiers nearby as he harnessed Pan to his sledge, himself crawling on the ground towards the group of wounded soldiers. Pan knew what he had to do and zigzagged after Fritz, pulling his sledge. They found two soldiers, one dead, the other badly wounded. Fritz put the bleeding soldier on the sleigh and Pan ran as fast as he could towards the camp, zigzagging under a hail of shots coming from the forest. He arrived safely, and von Riedler took care of the patient without looking at Pan, who was rather at a loss as to how to proceed. Then like lightning they could see him running back to find Fritz. They could see some wounded soldiers farther away and near the forest, but as they were still under heavy fire they did not have a chance of reaching them. It was as if Pan could read Fritz's thoughts: *You have a chance, being much faster and smaller than I.*

Pan now could put all his training to the test, zigzagging between Fritz and the enemy running at top speed. He reached an elderly soldier who had his left leg partly torn off, and another young soldier, bleeding from the forehead, helped the men up on the sledge.

Pan stood quite still for a few seconds to get his bearings and then started with a powerful jerk. The snow was cold, his paws freezing, but the sledge slid easily on the hard and icy surface. Pan ran towards the camp, not knowing whether his friends were covering him.

This time the baron had the time to pat him. "Remember, it is Christmas Eve and we shall have our wine bottle, so come back and don't stay out there," he said. "Now, run; run."

Fritz had in the meantime bandaged up another wounded man and was watching Pan returning to him from the camp. "Pan," he said softly, "I hate doing this to you, but you have to take this soldier back. It is your job; that's all."

Fritz put the soldier on the sledge, and Pan was off. Suddenly he felt a sharp pain in his right front paw and in his side. He also felt that the bullets hit the sledge. He continued running, but at a lower speed. He heard a hissing sound in front of him and knew it meant danger. He took a sharp turn to the left and ran for his life. The explosion did not hurt him, but the soldiers watching the incident were terrified as they were sure that Pan had got it this time. They all had to admire this dog and what he had done, and when they saw Pan arriving at the camp from the west side they all cheered him. They lifted the wounded soldier from the sledge, but he was dead, pierced through by bullets. They saw Pan bleeding from his wounds, but before they could see to him he was off again.

"Come back, Pan; come back!" they all cried.

But Pan would not stop. He felt the pain, but he also felt that he had to go back to Fritz, to whom he was very attached. He was now very tired and rested his head in Fritz's lap.

"Poor old Pan, and you are wounded." Fritz bandaged up Pan's paw and let him rest for a while. Then he said, "I hate to ask you, but this will be your last job today; I promise you." He went over to a small dark man and felt his pulse. "If we are to save this man, you shall have to go now. And don't come back. We shall manage somehow to get back to the camp." He saw Pan limping and zigzagging towards the camp.

Pan was completely exhausted and it all blanked out before his eyes. He stumbled forward and fainted on reaching the camp.

The baron removed the splinter of a shell from Pan's paw and stitched the wound.

"What about the wound in the side?" asked the other doctors. "Let's stitch it up."

"Don't stitch!" shouted the baron. "Don't stitch, you idiots!"

Now he has really gone mad, they thought.

"Don't you even know, you who are supposed to be doctors, that if you stitch a boxer's coat you will leave a scar forever? I shall have Pan on show after the war."

They all stared at him and could not believe what they heard. These dogs were never kept alive for more than a few months. They saw the baron carefully bandaging up Pan's right side, lifting him up, and carrying him away as if he were a newborn baby.

"Quite out of his senses," one said, "but what a doctor."

Some hours had passed and the area had quieted down. Pan was lying resting on the sofa, and there was a bottle of wine on the table.

Pan woke up hearing some voices outside the tent.

"You will celebrate Christmas as planned," the baron told them. "Tidy up the place and collect some brandy from the cook."

"Where do we bury the dead?" one asked.

"Wait until tomorrow and you can bury them together with those from the hospital. How many were killed by the fire?"

"Twenty-three."

"Twenty-three," repeated the baron in a mild voice. "Don't touch anything until the fire has gone completely out."

Black smoke arose from the ruins, giving off a sour and unpleasant smell.

The baron was busy on the phone, which had been connected up again.

Pan rested quietly whilst he was listening to his master and suddenly got the surprise of his life when he saw the cook. He thought the cook had died and could not believe his own eyes. To be quite sure, he touched the cook with his paw and sniffed. Finally he was convinced and wagged his tail and the cook patted him on the head.

"Yes, it is me," he said smiling. "I was only thrown to the ground and the wind knocked out of me for a short while." He showed Pan a large tray of meat. "This is from me and the boys," he said and started feeding Pan with his own hands. Although Pan was tired, he found the meat most delicious and had eaten half the portion when he had to say stop, as he was full up.

"We will save the rest till tomorrow," said the cook. "I'll put the tray under the sofa." He took up a bottle from his pocket and finished what was left of his Christmas ration.

The baron stood right behind him. "Dismissed!" he shouted.

The cook got up and the baron handed him a fresh bottle. "This is a present from Pan," he said, smiling. It was the first time the cook had seen the baron smile, and he limped happily, and a little tight, back to his kitchen.

The baron put a match to the small candle and poured some wine into the glass on the table.

CHAPTER

FOUR

Oslo—*Christmas Eve*

Anne lit the large candlesticks in the large dining room, which was decorated for Christmas. The tree was placed in the lounge, and as usual the professor sat at his grand piano playing Christmas carols. Laila sat by the fire, the flames giving a soft light to her face and light-coloured hair. She went across to the big red ball and kissed it.

She did not notice that her father had stopped playing. He said in a sad voice: "Laila, Pan is dead. He is with your mother now."

Laila turned around quickly and said in a hard tone: "Pan is not dead; I can feel he is alive. And he is thinking of me now this very minute."

"Come let us eat," her father said mildly.

They went into the dining room, where Anne was waiting for them.

Outside, the snow was falling, covering the trees, streets, and roofs.

Norway was occupied. People were frightened and sad at the news of more brave Norwegians being shot or sent to concentration camps. Many had lost a close relative over the year, and their thoughts went to these men and women and also to those fighting the enemy from England and overseas, but Laila's thoughts were with Pan. She did not cry over Pan anymore; she only dreamed about him. Night and day Pan was always with her. She took a small candle and placed it next to the ball.

She peeked out of the window. The snow had covered everything just like a quiet, comforting carpet trying to alleviate the sorrow and ease the pain.

Germany

The moon was shining, throwing a yellowish light over the park and all the bronze sculptures. The baroness sat as usual on Christmas Eve at the piano and played her favourite Christmas carols. Her thoughts went to her only son, Otto. There were no guests at the estate this Christmas, apart from the tenant farmer and family. The butler announced that dinner was ready and the two old people went arm in arm and sat down at the beautiful table, decorated for the occasion with all the silver heirlooms.

Eastern front

The soldiers also celebrated their Christmas. They enjoyed the extra ration and talked about all the friends they had lost that day. They sat there all together in a large tent, tired and plastered, most of them. They all remembered Pan and toasted him. They all felt they owned a part of him, and they loved him. The night was black with no moon.

There was no sound from the baron's tent. He only sat there with Pan in his lap, rocking the dog to sleep. Otto had some wine in his glass but did not touch it. He was tired after a strenuous day, and his thoughts went to his parents and all the beautiful Christmas Eves they had spent together. He remembered the tall Christmas trees they always had, especially picked out by him in the estate's forest. He remembered the large table and all the relatives present dressed up to celebrate. He remembered his grey-haired mother playing the piano and started humming "O Holy Night."

Pan woke up and watched his friend. He listened to him and was somewhat amazed. He had never expected his friend to be able to sing. The baron kept rocking, however, and soon Pan went back to sleep.

The Germans suffered heavy losses now, and wounded soldiers were taken care of day and night. The doctors were worn out and their nerves on edge. Besides the baron and the cook, Fritz was Pan's real friend and comrade. Fritz was his boss out in the field, and Pan understood that. But he also knew that the baron was his master, and Pan loved the baron and was also very fond of the cook. When Fritz and he were alone Fritz always took up his wallet and showed Pan a photo of a handsome girl with light hair. Pan loved to look at this photo; she was so much like Laila. It made him sad and glad at the same time.

"I can see you like her," Fritz said. "I know it; I can see it in your eyes. You like blonde girls like I do. And this is not just any girl; it is my young wife. After the war you shall meet her. I promise you."

One day when Pan and Fritz, as usual, sat in the tent warming up next to the stove, the baron entered and told them he had a job for them to do. He pulled up a map from his side pocket, pointed, and explained, "One of our troops while scouting has been ambushed by the partisans and has been chased up the hill here. There are several wounded. You have to get round the hill and up the pass here, and you will find our men."

"But surely we are no mountain climbers," Fritz protested.

"You are from now on," said the baron, and continued, "They have some important documents they were supposed to surrender to General Mann; you must get hold of the documents."

Fritz collected all his gear, medicine, rope, and ammunition, and harnessed Pan to the sledge, and together they left the camp and proceeded towards their destination. It was cold and icy and the sledge glided easily on this surface. They consulted the map and compass, and after several hours they could see the mountain far away.

"We must be there before dark," Fritz told Pan.

They had a short rest and helped themselves to some food and then were off again. They finally started the actual climbing. The mountainside was steep and the surface very rugged, and it was a strenuous job to pull the sledge. It also jammed several times, and Fritz had to help Pan get the sledge loose when it got stuck between ice and rock. They found a ledge where they sat down to rest when all of a sudden the sledge started sliding, pulling Pan back. Pan was whining, and Fritz got hold of his collar, frantically trying to hold back, but all in vain; the sledge was now hanging in the empty air over the cliff.

Fritz managed to get his feet against a rock, thus stopping any further slipping, but he realised that there was no chance of saving Pan and the sledge, so he resolutely picked up his knife and after several efforts managed to cut Pan loose, pulling him back to a safer place. Fritz was completely exhausted and out of breath, and he heard with a shudder the sledge being crushed deep down at the bottom of the cliff.

"I would never have given you up, Pan," he said. "I would rather have gone down with you."

Pan understood that Fritz had saved his life. They had to get on with the job assigned to them, and after some climbing they reached the area that should be the area in which they could find the soldiers. It was getting darker now, and after another quarter of an hour's search they hit upon the troop. Two were unhurt, one had been shot in the leg, and the fourth was badly off, having lost a lot of blood. They were all tired and frostbitten. The snow was coloured red, and Fritz tucked the badly wounded man in the only blanket he had and gave the badly wounded a dose of morphia. Fritz explained to them that he had had to give up the sledge. "I can get the three of you down from this place by using a western route, and some soldiers from my unit will meet us there tomorrow, so we shall wait here awhile.

"As for you," he addressed the badly wounded man, "we shall need a stretcher to get you back, but how?" He looked at Pan. "Can you find the way back to the camp, Pan? You have no weight or sledge to pull, and you should make it in half the time we took getting here."

He sat down, found a small pencil, and wrote on a scrap of paper:

Sledge lost. Request assistance west side of mountain. Stretcher needed for one badly wounded. Sledge impossible, too steep.

F.

He put the note in a small leather pouch, which he tied securely to Pan's collar. "Run, Pan; run to the baron."

And Pan was off. He did not like it, thinking of the cliffs, but was pleasantly surprised when he realised how much easier it was to travel when he had nothing to pull or carry.

After some time he rested for a short while, turned his head to get his bearings, and noticed that someone was watching him: enemy soldiers standing right behind him. Pan had seen the uniform before on dead soldiers and on prisoners.

Pan got very frightened, but an inner voice told him not to try anything stupid.

"It is a German dog. There must be Germans around here somewhere, you can see the Red Cross on the collar. Don't shoot the dog; he will lead us to the enemy tomorrow, and we can ambush them."

They put some blankets around themselves and sat down. Pan hoped that it would become darker and kept quiet.

"It is, no doubt, a smart dog, but we shall outsmart him," one said and lit a pipe.

Suddenly, with a big jump, Pan ran as fast as he could towards a clump of trees. The soldiers had practically dozed off but were now on their feet chasing him. Pan used his last resources of strength and reached the trees. He started digging frantically with his paws. When he finally got through the snow crust the rest was easy, as the snow under the crust was soft and powdery. He managed to dig deep enough to hide himself when he heard voices nearby. Pan kept completely quiet and tried to hold his breath as much as possible. They passed only a few yards away from him, and Pan was terrified.

"Damn that bloody dog! He has completely disappeared; we should have shot him right away," someone said. "Anyhow, we cannot stay here all night; we better get back. Damn that dog," he repeated.

Pan kept quiet for quite some time, and after a while, feeling more relaxed, he got up, shook the snow off his coat, and tried to get his bearings. The moon was now shining, it was very cold, and he started running. The snow crust was strong enough to bear his weight, and he made extremely good speed. At last he could see his camp as a dark shadow far away. Pan felt very happy and barked with joy. He was still barking when he reached the camp and his friends, having heard his barking for quite some time, were out to meet him.

"Where did you come from, and where is Fritz?" the baron asked Pan in a shaky voice. The thought of losing Pan terrified him. He saw the leather pouch, took Pan inside the tent, and read the short note from Fritz. He called an officer to get in touch with a troop of soldiers nearby to pick up Fritz and the wounded men.

"Fritz will hopefully be here tomorrow," he told Pan. "And now, Pan, you'd better tell me your adventure and tell the cook as well," the baron said as the cook entered with some food.

Pan started growling, digging in a piece of rug on the ground, and then hid himself underneath. There he was completely quiet, looking at the baron with watchful eyes. After a while he went back to his sofa, opened his mouth, and showed his white teeth and smiled.

The baron and the cook were

shrieking with laughter, the cook's eyes full of tears and the baron nearly losing his breath. Several others heard the commotion and entered, asking what it was all about. Pan started a repeat performance, and they were all laughing.

"There must be some partisans around here," one said in a low voice. "We'd better send out a warning."

Fritz and the others arrived in camp safely the following day, and Fritz was exceedingly grateful to see Pan again, safe and sound.

The German army was driven back on all fronts, and Baron Otto von Riedler received orders to break camp and pull back farther west. It was cold and the road icy and bumpy. Most of the villages they passed were burnt down and empty of people. After several days they arrived at a village with some houses intact and established the new field hospital. Wounded soldiers arrived every day, keeping the baron busy day and night. Also Pan and Fritz were fully occupied in their job collecting and helping the wounded.

There were practically no dogs from the Medical Corps alive, and Pan, who was on the job every day, had become a living legend. He could even all by himself manage to bring wounded to the hospital when Fritz was busy somewhere else. And no one could tell how many lives Pan had saved.

One day the baron showed Fritz a map and indicated with his finger a particular spot. "Here a medical officer and his men have been wounded and possibly killed in an ambush. I do not know what can be done, but I want you to take Pan and an army officer and see if there is anything to be done. Take Peter—you have worked with him before—and tell him to report to me as soon as you arrive."

71

They left and reached their destination without any difficulties. It was a distressful and tragic sight. They were all dead. Pan studied the face of a young fair-haired boy whom he remembered so well from his first training camp. He was dead, and next to him sat Bambi, her chest spattered with blood. She sat quite still with her one eye staring in front of her.

"My God," said Fritz, fixed and motionless with horror at the sight of the boxer and the boy. Fritz lifted the wounded boxer in his arms and placed her on the sledge.

"I shall help you pushing; the snow is heavy now, nearing spring."

Fritz nearly cried; he did not know why. It must have been the sight of this dying boxer. *What will Pan think, seeing man's cruelty?*

Pan started barking hysterically, pulling Bambi and the sledge along the road. Faster and faster he ran, and the other two could not keep pace with him and finally he disappeared. But they could hear his barking through the thin air. His surroundings going black in front of his eyes, Pan reached the camp, collided with a soldier, stopped abruptly in front of the surgery, and kept on barking and howling. The baron ran out to meet him, as he heard the fear and pain in Pan's voice and saw the little boxer lying on the sledge, dead.

The baron lifted the small boxer, the blood staining his coat, while the cook was patting Pan, trying to comfort him. But Pan kept on howling. Fritz released the sledge and the baron put the little boxer on a small rug, Pan sitting next to his Bambi, licking her continuously as if trying to bring her back to life. He had stopped howling now, only uttering some peculiar soft sad sobs.

"Poor Pan, he must have got a shock seeing one of his own race dying," Fritz said.

Neither the baron nor Fritz knew that the small boxer lying there shot to pieces was Pan's great and unforgettable love. The cook tried to give him some food, but Pan did not touch it.

"My dear Pan, I am sorry I cannot bring the dead boxer back to life. There is nothing I would rather do, but she is dead, Pan, just like many of your other friends," the baron said. "Let us go to bed," continued the baron. "It is getting dark." But Pan went instead out in the cold and with Fritz sat down outside the surgery. The night was dark, but soon the moon appeared. Pan started howling towards the sky, breaking the silence. The baron heard him from his tent, the cook sitting next to his stove, and all the soldiers. And Pan kept on howling, tears running down his cheeks. He was completely broken-hearted.

The baron came out with a spade, saying to Fritz, "Let us dig a grave for the little boxer; it might make Pan feel better."

They allowed Pan to lick his little boxer good-bye and after burying her went quietly back to the tent. The baron gave Pan an injection, and Pan went off to sleep very quickly. In his sleep, his body was shaking and tears welled up in his eyes. The cook came in and sat down. He had forgotten all about discipline and helped himself to some coffee without offering any to the baron.

"I cannot even cry," said the cook. "But why couldn't God let Pan keep this little boxer he found?"

Fritz went unhappily back to his own tent. He could not sleep, however. Something had been broken inside him.

Days became weeks and the weather improved.

"I think I prefer the cold winter to all this mud and wet snow," Fritz said to the baron one day, "and it is a very heavy job to pull the sledge."

"We have just received orders to move farther east, and maybe we shall also get some leave," the baron answered, "but in the meantime you have to take a last trip to collect some of those wounded by an air attack. I shall give you further information when you are ready."

Fritz felt very happy. At last they would leave this muddy place and move nearer home.

They went eastwards and after some time found the soldiers scattered around on the ground, a few wounded but most of them dead. Fritz was just giving one of the wounded morphia when they saw two enemy fighter planes come roaring towards them.

"Seek cover!" Fritz shouted to Pan, at the same covering the wounded with his body. Pan heard only the roaring from the engines as he stretched out close to the ground next to a dead soldier.

Fritz woke up, as if after a nightmare, when he heard the planes disappearing. Then he discovered that he was wounded. He lay on the ground twisting his body. Pan ran up to him as Fritz called him in a choked voice.

"Run, Pan, run," he said as he managed to get the wounded soldier on the sledge, "run, and come back for me."

But for the first time Pan did not obey. He looked at Fritz with pleading eyes as if saying, "You, Fritz, I want to take you to the baron first, please, Fritz."

"No, Pan, you have to take the wounded soldier now and come back for me; you have to. Pan, run; run."

Pan realised that it was only a waste of time arguing with Fritz and started on his way back to the hospital. He turned his head several times and saw Fritz sitting against a tree trunk holding his hand to his breast. Pan ran as fast as he could back to the camp, and the baron lifted the wounded soldier from the sledge, but he was already dead.

Immediately Pan turned back to pick up Fritz. It was darker now, and in the twilight Pan had to search for some time before he found Fritz sitting up against the tree. Pan looked at him in astonishment and despair. Fritz was dead. Pan lay down close to him and felt the loneliness more intensely than ever before, just like the first night in Germany and the night Bambi died. And now his dear friend Fritz was gone too.

Pan felt Fritz's body getting colder, but he still kept close to him. He did not howl this time. He did not look towards the sky. For Pan there was no heaven anymore.

From the camp they had started retreating westwards, and the baron was sitting in his tent alone. He went out from time to time looking for Pan and Fritz and finally left the camp to look for them. It was a rather tough job for him, not being used to this form of exercise. He reached the place where he saw the dead soldiers, but no Fritz or Pan. He searched farther afield and finally noticed something brown in colour against a tree. He realised it was Pan and walked across to him. He was not in a hurry anymore; he just stood watching Pan sitting close to his dead friend. The baron sat down on Fritz's other side for a long time without saying a word. He finally took Fritz's wallet and took off his ring. He fastened the ring to Pan's collar and said, "Say good-bye to your friend, Pan."

But Pan did not move.

They heard the fighter planes coming back and both had to seek cover under some bushes. When it was safe, they got up and started returning. The camp was practically empty of men now, and they joined the last lot leaving the camp for their next destination, which they reached without any incident five days later.

After a few days in the new camp a big transport plane arrived and they all went aboard. The baron watched his men. Fourteen men were all he had left; the rest were all dead, apart from a few badly wounded who had been sent back home. It was spring now and the countryside looked rather pretty, but they all cursed the place and were glad to leave. The engines roared and Pan looked at all the men. They were all his friends, and the men felt that Pan belonged to each one of them. Pan had his big black eyes fixed on all of them and noticed how old and worn they all looked, although most of them were only young men.

CHAPTER

FIVE

Berlin

It was a strange feeling for Otto von Riedler to arrive in Berlin after such a long time. He said good-bye to his small troop, and Pan wagged his tail as they all patted him.

"We shall see you again," said the cook optimistically, mostly to himself. He wanted to take Pan with him here and now.

"Come on Pan," said the baron, saluted the others, and left the airport. They jumped on a bus, and the other passengers had to admire the dog, with springing muscles and shining coat. They could all see he was well trained. They should only have known how Pan had got his training. Pan himself felt strong as a lion and returned their staring with his dreamy black eyes.

They passed a number of houses in ruins and finally reached their destination, left the bus, and went across the street and entered the garden surrounding a charming white house. "I had better use the bell," the baron said to Pan. "Otherwise we will scare the life out of her, if she is still here." They heard heavy steps and saw an old face watching them with consternation and joy.

"Otto!"

The baron put his arms around the heavy old body and kissed her on the cheek and said time and time again, "Dear, dear old nanny."

Pan stood quite still, watching, until the baron remembered him. "This is Pan, my best friend," he said, patting the dog on the head.

"Where did you get this dog?" she wanted to know.

"He is the only survivor from the front; all the others died."

"Oh, is that the case?" she said quietly. "You know your father had to give away all his dogs, don't you?"

Yes, Otto knew that and he felt very sorry for his father, knowing how much he loved his dogs. Actually, the baron was very much attached to his father, although he did not like to admit it. He did not want to get involved, but the war had perhaps made him a little softer. Of one thing he was sure, however; he loved his friend Pan.

They entered the house and went upstairs to Otto's room with the old nanny behind them groaning heavily. It was a large room furnished in heavy oak, but what impressed Pan more than anything else was a large baldachin bed richly carved. Pan had never seen such a bed before, but he realised they were going to sleep in it and with a jump he was in the bed, walking around enjoying himself.

Nanny went downstairs to prepare some food, and they had their meal in the hall on the ground floor. Pan really enjoyed his food, and when they had finished they went down in the cellar where the baron collected some bottles of wine and carried them upstairs in a basket.

The baron was phoning some of his friends, and Pan sat close to him. He also phoned his father and mother, who lived down at the estate. The baron sounded very happy, making Pan also feel happy. They went upstairs to Otto's room, and the baron picked up some old gramophone records and started to play. Pan was back in bed again and listened attentively. He was quite sure that Laila soon would turn up, and his eyes turned dreamy.

"You have obviously heard this kind

of music before," Otto said to Pan. "We shall play some more."

The doorbell interrupted the music. Otto went downstairs, opening the door, and Pan heard a voice he knew he had heard before. Pan ran down the stairs and saw Kurt Zimmermann standing in the hall next to the baron. Pan nearly passed out, and so did Kurt Zimmermann.

"My God!" he exclaimed as Pan was jumping on him. Kurt put out his arms around Pan, hugging him. "Pan, Pan, you are alive," he panted while Pan was jumping on him, whimpering and whining.

Coffee and the last bottle of brandy were served in the hall, Pan keeping the men company.

"Please tell me more about Pan," Kurt Zimmermann pleaded.

And the baron told him. Pan knew they were talking about him, and he felt in seventh heaven in the company of his two friends.

The baron recounted the incident when Pan came back to the camp with another wounded boxer and also about Pan's behaviour when this small boxer died.

"We buried her," the baron said finally, "but even I felt very unhappy at that time."

A strange feeling arose in Kurt Zimmermann, and he asked the baron, "What did she look like, this little boxer?"

"She did not look at all," answered the baron. "She had only one eye and large, ugly scars all over her body." Suddenly he discovered his old friend staring at him, his face in deathly pallor, his hand holding the glass shaking and spilling brandy on the carpet.

"What is the matter?" the baron enquired, somewhat disturbed. "Do you feel ill?"

Kurt Zimmermann pulled himself together, put his glass on the table, and started talking about the little boxer, Bambi, the most beautiful boxer he had ever seen. He told the baron about Pan's love and affection for his Bambi and how Pan had saved her from an Alsatian belonging to an SS officer.

"I should never have sent Bambi to the front. It would have been better to let her die after the incident with the Alsatian. She was in a very bad state."

The baron looked at Pan and felt very sorry for him, having found his dear one and having to watch her die. He cursed the war and the whole mad world, filled the glasses, and said, "Let us try to be happy, Kurt. We never know whether we shall meet again. And you are off to the front. A toast to Pan and Bambi."

It was getting late, and Kurt had to leave. He patted Pan and shook hands with his friend Otto, went back to Pan, hugging him closely, and left the room. They heard the heavy door closing and the sound of his disappearing steps. It was the last time they saw Kurt Zimmermann.

Otto von Riedler now worked in the military hospital in Berlin, awaiting his leave, which was due in a month's time. He was busy in the surgery every day and was admired by the younger surgeons for his skill performing operations that at that time were considered impossible. Thus he saved considerable lives that were practically written off as hopeless cases. All his colleagues wanted to get closer to him, but he was not interested and when he had finished for the day he went quietly home to Pan and Nanny. Every night he took Pan for a walk and Pan knew where they would end up, in the small local nightclub. It had been a very smart place before the war, and the baron was well

known there. The old and smiling barkeeper always asked him about his
family, whom he had known for many
years. And Otto told him what he knew
and that he was going down to the
estate shortly.

"You have a beautiful dog there,"
the barkeeper said, admiring Pan. "Is
he from your father's kennel?"

"Yes," lied the baron.

The barkeeper noticed a number of
women in the bar, obviously interested
in the baron, trying their old tricks to
get acquainted, but the baron had only
eyes for Pan and gave him beer, a drink
that Pan had acquired a taste for and
appreciated. It was just as if these two
had a big secret together, and somehow
it irritated some of the other guests.

One day the baron said to Pan, "We
are not going to the bar today; we are
going somewhere else."

They caught a taxi and travelled
right through Berlin. Everywhere there

were bombed-out houses. The baron told the driver to stop when they arrived at a big apartment block. They went down a long corridor and the baron had to check the names on the doors before he found what he was looking for and pressed the bell.

It took some time before the door was opened. Appearing in the doorway was a quite young woman with fair hair, saying "How do you do?"

"My name is Otto von Riedler," he said, stretching out his hand.

"Please come in," she said, grasping his hand. Then she suddenly discovered Pan and retreated a few steps. "My God," she whispered, "this must be Fritz' dog." She patted Pan and kissed his head tenderly, as if he were a small child. And soft tears ran down her cheeks. "Please come in." She led Pan by his leash and stood admiring him, completely fascinated. "You are really beautiful, just like Fritz described you in the few letters that reached me from the front. Please sit down," she said to the baron, pointing to a small settee. It was a small apartment, but clean and cosy. On a desk were photos of Fritz. The young woman had blue eyes, and her skin was soft. She was dressed in a nurse's uniform, slim and well built, and the baron found her very attractive. Out of his pocket he took Fritz's brown wallet. Momentarily Pan grabbed the wallet and held it between his teeth as if to emphasize that it belonged to him.

"But, Pan!" the baron exclaimed.

But Pan did not give in. He recognised the woman from the photo Fritz had shown him and after a while felt a little stupid, but he took the little brown wallet and placed it in her lap.

She patted the dog and pressed the wallet against her breast.

"Crying is allowed," the baron said.

But she did not cry anymore, just kept on patting the dog.

Pan felt extremely sorry for her. Then she noticed the engagement ring on Pan's chain.

"Give it to her, Pan; it belongs to her."

The baron tried to explain. "You understand, Pan would not leave until I gave him this ring."

"Please tell me the whole story," she pleaded.

"I was searching for Pan and Fritz, but I found only Pan alive, as I wrote to you in my letter."

She nodded. "So Pan was with Fritz when he died?" she asked anxiously.

"Yes, they sat close together against a tree."

"Thank God. Then Fritz was not alone when he died. He had his dear friend close to him. I am very relieved and grateful. Fritz said always that dying all alone must be terrible. Let Pan keep the ring, and he shall always remember Fritz."

She brought some coffee and they talked quietly together and Pan had never seen the baron so relaxed before. Pan knew instinctively that his master had fallen for this kind and attractive woman.

"I am afraid we shall have to go." Finally the baron got up from the settee. "You must come and visit Pan; I believe Fritz would have liked that." He gave her his card.

"Maybe one day." She nodded, caressing Pan.

The baron shook her hand and said in what was for him a very mild voice: "Auf Wiedersehen."

Once they were outside, the baron said, "Let us pay a last visit to our nightclub, because tomorrow we shall go down to the estate with Nanny."

The baron had a short drink, but he obviously did not enjoy the patrons that particular night, so he and Pan left the bar. They had just walked a few hundred yards when they heard the air-raid warning, followed by an explosion, a bomb hitting a house close by. Pan was thrown many yards down the street by the pressure, and several minutes passed before he came to and managed to free himself of all the dust and plaster covering his coat. He stood there half-blinded in the dark and started barking. He ran up and down the street trying to find the baron. The area was full of smoke and dust, and Pan ran desperately around trying to trace his master, barking all the time.

At last he heard the baron call out to him. "Pan, Pan!"

He ran towards the burning house, found his master lying under some debris, and tried to free him. But the baron was stuck, his one leg completely trapped by an iron beam. He was in great pain and fainted several times, and Pan tried to comfort him by licking his forehead and cheek. The fire drew closer and Pan was really frightened and started digging around the beam, but to no avail. Poor Pan did not know what to do, but suddenly he made up his mind and ran towards the nightclub.

On reaching the bar Pan got hold of the barkeeper's trousers and dragged him towards the door. But the barman did not want to leave the premises and refused to go with Pan.

"Hold on!" one of the guests cried out. "Something must have happened to the baron. He and his dog left just a few minutes before the air raid. It is quiet outside now; let us take a stretcher and go out looking for him. Any volunteers?" He looked around him. "I shall go; who else?" he said.

A bar assistant came forward, and together they followed Pan and found the baron lying helplessly amongst the ruins. He was covered by blood and dust, but they managed to get him loose and carefully carried him to the stretcher. They examined his bleeding leg and realised the baron was very badly wounded. They managed to hail an ambulance down the street. Pan jumped in to be with the baron.

"Get out of here," the baron shouted to him. "Get out of here and go back to Nanny."

But Pan did not move.

The baron feared that somebody, the Wehrmacht maybe, would take Pan away from him and send him back to the front.

"Put him to sleep." The baron asked the ambulance driver to help him, and almost immediately Pan fell asleep. They dragged him out of the car.

"I am very grateful to you," the baron thanked his two rescuers, "and please see to it that my dog gets home somehow." Then he passed out.

Nanny always stayed down in the

cellar during an air raid and was half asleep when she was awakened by a terrific banging on the front door. She ran upstairs, opened the door, and saw Pan lying there immovable.

"What has happened?" she cried out.

"The baron is wounded and here is the dog." They explained to her that the baron was injured and had been driven by ambulance to a hospital, that his leg was in a bad state but otherwise he was all right.

"But what about the dog?" Nanny asked.

"Oh, the dog will be all right in a few hours. The baron gave him an injection," they comforted her.

"Please, carry the dog upstairs; he is too heavy for me." Nanny looked at them with pleading eyes.

They put him in the baron's bed, the two rescuers being very impressed by the enormous bed.

They heard the all-clear signal and left the house, Nanny following them to the front door, thanking them warmly for their help.

The baron was operated on not once, but several times, and they succeeded in saving his leg. He had to stay in the hospital for many weeks, and Nanny came to see him every day. Every time the baron enquired about Pan and got the same answer; Pan was locked up in the house when she left, but all the same he was always inside the garden gate waiting for her to come back from the hospital. But the baron knew how Pan got out, through the cellar window, an escape route he himself had used when he was a boy.

One day Nanny told Pan that the following day they were travelling south to the estate. There was too much bombing now in Berlin, and the baron thought it safer for them to stay with his parents. Nanny went to the hospital for the last time to say good-bye to the baron.

"What are you going to do without us?" she asked. "I understand you must stay here for several months yet."

"Don't worry about me," the baron answered, "I shall write a book, a book about Pan. I want all the world to know about this unique dog. I think I shall call it, *The Dog from the North*."

Nanny said to him almost in a whisper: "Do not worry about Pan. I shall look after him, and I hope to see you soon down at the estate."

She turned at the door, waving, and the nurse could see she was crying. The old nanny was very attached to the baron. She went quickly back to see Pan.

CHAPTER

SIX

It was a long train journey. Nanny was feeding Pan from an old bag, and Pan was sitting next to her. The train was overcrowded, and the passengers watching Pan found him both snobbish and arrogant. It was obvious that Pan had taken after his master.

At last, after many hours, Nanny got up and, taking Pan by the lead, got off the train. It was a small, rather cosy railway station. On the platform Otto's father was waiting for them in his car. He was not as tall as Otto, but otherwise they looked very much alike. He greeted Nanny and patted Pan on his head. They drove through the countryside and finally left the main road; some distance away Pan could see a large white house. Brackenweld looked like a small castle and was surrounded by a large park.

"Come with me, Pan."

Pan followed the baron's father, keeping close to him.

"I want you to meet Otto's mother."

She was small, dark, and very attractive. "My dear Pan," she said, "Otto has written so much about you."

Pan was sitting right in front of her chair and looked at her with his dreamy black eyes.

"Our little Pan," she whispered, "our little Pan."

The days went by, and the weeks, and although Pan was enjoying his stay at the castle, where they were all very kind to him, he was longing for his master and for hours he could just sit quietly staring out in the air thinking about him.

So one day the old baron told Pan

to jump in the car and with himself in the driver's seat they drove on the narrow, bumpy road, and on reaching the main road Pan knew instinctively that that his master was coming back to him.

They reached the station and had to wait a few hours, as the train was delayed.

Finally the overcrowded train arrived and Pan could see one person leaving the train, limping as he walked towards them, the baron, Pan's master.

With a terrific jump Pan landed on the baron with his eighty pounds. The baron just managed to keep on his feet. He laughed loudly and held Pan close to him. He freed himself from Pan after a while and greeted his father warmly. Pan was running around them in circles and felt he had never been so happy before.

The baron still had awful pains in his leg and walked with a pronounced limp, as the leg was too weak to carry any weight.

"My poor boy," the baroness said to herself, seeing her son dragging himself along, but actually she was glad. *This is our salvation,* she thought. *They will not send him back to the front now.*

The baron's leg gradually improved, and he took Pan for walks in the garden. They also did some fishing in a small river running through the grounds, and Pan was always fascinated when the baron caught a fish. Otherwise the baron spent most of his time on the terrace in the shade, writing. And Pan was always there with him, playing around.

"Tell me about the front," the father one night asked his son.

"There is nothing to tell," answered Otto. "Blood and death, that is what I shall remember. Otherwise I have nothing to tell. The whole war is hell and absolutely meaningless."

"Don't talk in that way," his father said warningly. "Quite a few have been arrested lately for similar utterances."

"It certainly is hell," continued Otto. "We have lost all the dogs, horses, and a number of friends. But I have been lucky in a way, having my best friend still with me." He looked at Pan with a warm smile.

The Germans suffered heavy losses on all fronts and called up all their reserves. Otto von Riedler received the telegram he had feared for some time; this time he was ordered to the western front. Otto kissed his mother good-bye, and together with his father he drove to the small railway station, where they had to part. The old baron felt extremely sad and left the station in his car before the train arrived.

Pan felt the strained atmosphere and stayed close to his master in the overcrowded train. He realised that they were going back to the front, and his thoughts went to Bambi and Fritz. He trembled in spite of the warm spring, and the baron suddenly regretted bringing Pan with him, as they were both so attached to each other.

"Come back, both of you!" were the old baron's last words to his son.

It was a long and unpleasant trip, but finally they could leave the train and proceed by truck. They arrived at a small field hospital and were greeted by an old doctor, the only doctor left in the camp.

"This will be exactly the same as on the eastern front," the baron said to himself, "blood, hard work, and death."

The air attacks continued day and night, and the Medical Corps had great losses.

"This is hopeless," Otto von Riedler told a general on inspection. "This is suicide. We send out ten of our troops to pick up wounded. They return with maybe three wounded; at the same time we lose five of our men. Very soon there won't be anyone left here from the Medical Corps."

"It is an order," the general said shortly and drove off.

For the baron everything was only routine. His bad leg was a big handicap in his work, and quite frequently he had to sit on a high chair to relieve the strain on the leg.

Pan was on his old job again, picking up wounded, but this time he did it alone, as Fritz was dead and there was no one to replace him. It was a tough job pulling the sledge, but usually there was someone around to give a hand when required.

The bombing grew more and more intense, and the situation could have been chaotic if not for the iron will of the baron.

One day after a heavy air attack, Pan was sitting in front of the surgery when an SS officer arrived, slightly wounded. Pan, remembering this officer all too well, blocked the entrance and started snarling. The other men present were staring at Pan, dumbfounded. This was not at all like their Pan. But Pan was making a stand against the man, raising his hackles and growling with open mouth, baring his teeth.

"Oh, it is you again!" the officer shouted. "You are still alive, you brute, but we shall soon fix you." He drew his pistol, but it was immediately knocked out of his hand by the baron, who had heard Pan's growling and rushed to the place.

"Keep away from the dog, and after we have seen to you also keep away from my premises. That is an order." The baron was in a rage.

"You shall pay for this, you bloody aristocrat!" shouted the farm boy from Bayern. After being treated for his minor injuries, he left the hospital and went back to his position on top of a hill just east of the hospital, all the time planning his revenge.

All the men were amazed. They had never seen Pan behave in such a manner towards anybody. But they understood that there must be a reason for his attitude and they all patted him, trying to calm him down. Eventually Pan became more relaxed, at the same time waiting for his revenge.

The German troops were retreating all along the front and the field hospital was now in the line of fire and the baron commanded his men to leave and move farther eastward. He himself would stay behind looking after the wounded who were dying.

Pan and the baron were sitting by themselves in front of the tent. It was strangely quiet around them until Pan all of a sudden thought he heard footsteps. He snarled and turned around, but it was too late. He heard a shot and hoarse laughter and saw the back of a man running quickly towards the hill. Pan saw the baron faltering, crawling inside the tent. The dog could see the blood soaking his master's uniform and the baron's hands full of blood as he pressed them against his breast. Pan was in a state of perplexity and did not know what he should do. He watched his friend and master, completely lost, and saw his eyes changing in a strange way and remembered Fritz, how his eyes also became strange just before he died. Pan sat close to the baron and felt that his master took hold of his collar.

"He got us before the Allies," the baron whispered. "Go now, Pan, and give yourself up." Then he passed out.

Pan licked his forehead and now he finally realised what had happened. He was at a loss how to proceed, and he was full of hate. Suddenly he made up his mind. He got up and ran as fast as he could towards the top of the hill behind the hospital, where he knew there was a German machine-gun post. He was blinded by hate and sorrow and did not even notice the small Allied troop approaching behind him. He attacked the SS officer from behind, and together they tumbled down the hill. Pan felt an itching pain in the side, but even now he had not discovered the Allied troop watching this performance with amazement, completely fascinated. They saw the boxer finally managing to hold his opponent down on the ground and tear his throat. They could see the boxer making sure that his enemy was dead. Then he was off like lightning and disappeared into the forest. They called after him and they realised that the dog had saved their lives, as they would have been an easy target for the German machine-gun fire. They looked for the dog while they were advancing, but without any success. Pan had hidden under a big root and watched the troop. As soon as the way was clear he ran back to the field hospital and found it on fire. The blood was dripping from him, and he had a slight limp. He crawled into the small tent and sat close to his friend and master, the baron.

The baron woke up but was now very weak. He noticed Pan's wounds and held onto his collar. "So you got him at last, my friend," he whispered. With a last effort he held Pan close to him, patting his head feebly. After a while Pan could feel the grip loosen and the baron lay quite still. Otto von Riedler was dead.

The evening sun sent the last rays through the tent opening, and Pan could feel how the warmth left the baron's body, as he had experienced before with Bambi and Fritz. Pan's eyes were blinded with tears. He did not feel his own pain; he knew he was also going to die.

CHAPTER

SEVEN

A small group of American soldiers sat together celebrating V-E Day. They remembered the friends they had lost during the campaign and felt both happy and sad. They filled their glasses with beer and listened to Churchill speaking over the BBC. But they could not forget the beautiful brown boxer that in all probability had saved their lives. They all wondered what had happened to the dog.

"I cannot understand why a German dog should kill one of their own soldiers. There must have been a reason for it. And surely it was not to save our lives."

Harold, a dark-eyed boy, looked

around him, but as no one had any comments, he continued. "He was wounded, and he is probably lying dead somewhere out there, and this on the day of victory." He lit a cigarette and called the fair-haired waitress.

"What do you know about the golden boxer?"

She smiled. "Wehrmacht Hund."

"Of course," Harold exclaimed. "It is all clear now; it is an ambulance dog originally attached to the field hospital we passed. Come on, boys; we will take the jeep and look for our rescuer."

They returned to what was left of the field hospital and had a good look, but without finding the dog. Finally they discovered a small tent at the back of the camp apparently undamaged. They approached the tent carefully, fearing an ambush, and shouted, "Come out with your hands up!" But not a sound reached them apart from the evening breeze softly setting the tent cloth in motion.

Harold peeped carefully inside the tent and faced the boxer, Pan. He made a sign to the others to follow him, and they saw the baron sitting against the tent pole, dead, and in his hand he was holding onto a dog collar carrying the inscription: "Pan—Wehrmacht." His uniform was soaked with blood, and the dog was also covered in blood. The dog sat close to his master and did not move. The American soldiers were watching the scene speechlessly. In all its terror it was a very moving sight, a scene they knew would be printed in their memory forever. They saw two big black eyes full of tears, black tears. Pan was very weak and could just see the intruders through a haze.

They carried the dog to the jeep and drove to the hospital downtown, which had been taken over by the Allies.

Robert, the doctor, removed the

bullet but did not give the dog a chance to survive. "He must have a blood transfusion; that is our only hope. He has lost a great deal of blood."

"There must be a dog somewhere," Harold whispered. He and his friend Andrew went from house to house trying to find a dog, but without any success.

Suddenly, far down the street they saw an old woman with a rather shabby-looking dog walking behind her. They jumped in the jeep, started it up, and drove over to her and grabbed the dog. Shouting to the woman that they would be back with the dog soon, they drove back to the hospital at top speed.

"I have never done this before with dogs," Robert said, "but I know it will work and hopefully save your boxer."

They tapped the strange dog for the blood they wanted, and Andrew drove back to where they had left the old woman. She was sitting there on a bench softly crying, her eyes full of tears. Andrew thanked her for the loan of the dog and she managed a smile. She took the dog by the lead and more or less ran down the street, to safety.

They watched over Pan all the night, but there was no sign of improvement. There were a number of former prisoners from the Nazi concentration camps being treated at the hospital, among them a young Norwegian who was waiting for transport home. He had made friends with Harold and Andrew and told them about his life on the home front and his three years in a concentration camp. He was very thin and weak and in bad health. He joined his friends watching over Pan, patted the dog's head, and said in a low voice, "Poor little dog, you are not going to die, are you?"

Pan opened his black eyes and

looked at him. He tried to raise his head, but he was too weak.

"Did you see that? The dog reacts. Talk to him again in Norwegian," Andrew said eagerly.

They found a chair and the young Norwegian sat down next to Pan.

"I believe you understand Norwegian, my friend. How have you been able to survive all this time?" He kept on speaking softly to the dog, and after a while Pan managed to raise his head and rest it on the young man's arm.

"This we must celebrate. Get some brandy!" Andrew was very excited. "And thank you for saving the dog. I am sure he will be all right now," he continued, shaking hands with the Norwegian.

Pan's health improved quickly and after a few days he was able to walk around with his new friends.

They all cheered when they got the news that they were being stationed in Norway and they were all happy when they left the bombed-out ports in Germany.

That spring evening they were all together talking and Robert looked at Pan thoughtfully.

"That dog could tell us quite some stories. I wonder how long he has been in this war?"

"It cannot have been very long," Andrew said convincingly. "Remember all the dogs we have seen killed, either shot to pieces or mutilated by mines?"

"This dog is different," Robert insisted. "I don't know what it is, but that dog has certainly got something. I am sure he has been with his previous master, now dead, for several years."

Pan was sitting amongst them and knew they were talking about him. He also knew that they were all his friends and he had nothing to fear from any of them. He licked Harold's hand, and Harold had to agree with Robert that Pan was a kind of special dog.

"Pan," he said slowly, "Pan, a god. What a fitting name for him!"

The hours went by and it was early morning when they were sailing up the Oslo fjord. They were all on deck together with hundreds of other Allied troops. In the beginning they were met by Norwegian fishing boats running the Norwegian flag, the crews cheering. The soldiers waved at them. As they proceeded farther up the fjord they were met by hundreds of small boats cheering them enthusiastically grew, and as the fjord grew narrow they could observe all the small houses and gardens and thousands of Norwegians along the beach and Norwegian flags everywhere.

Pan stood motionless as a statue watching it all. His eyes grew larger and larger and blacker and blacker. The sun was shining, giving his coat a bronze tint. The soldiers looked at him, whispering, "He is not real."

They arrived in Oslo harbour about

midday, and after going ashore they were marching through the streets of Oslo, Pan in front as a mascot. The sidewalks were packed with people, young and old, all cheering their Allied friends, handing over flowers showing their appreciation and gratitude.

They must have had five long and terrible years, Robert thought. He waved back at the people and recorded this march through Oslo as the most fantastic thing he had ever experienced. It was a reception that would be in his memory forever.

Eventually they arrived at their destination, where they would be stationed temporarily, some barracks situated in the northern part of Oslo, previously occupied by German troops.

Some days after their arrival they were granted one day's leave, and after studying the tourist pamphlets that had been distributed to all Allied troops, they agreed to Robert's proposal. "We will go to Frogner Park and see the famous monuments and statues made by Vigeland. After that we shall go for a beer somewhere."

It was a pleasant afternoon. The lilacs were all abloom, and the park's flower beds flourished in all the colours of the rainbow. They crossed the bridge and watched the river sending cascades of water over the crocuses. They freed Pan from the lead and let him go loose. Pan looked around watchfully. He became quite alert, as if ready to attack. His body trembled and his eyes showed sudden recognition. All of a sudden Pan was off. They called him, but Pan kept running. They ran after him through the large gate in wrought iron and out in the street. They ran up and down the street shouting and calling his name, but Pan had completely vanished.

They asked everybody they met whether they had seen a brown boxer, but the answers were always in the negative. They walked down an adjoining street, and at last they found an elderly man who had actually observed a boxer entering a garden gate just down the road. He pointed at a large white house, and when they arrived they could see Pan standing on the steps in front of the entrance door. He was trembling all over. The door opened slowly, and an attractive fair girl appeared in the doorway. She stretched out her arms, and Pan jumped up with his forelegs around her neck. They were both crying. Her father heard the commotion and came outside. He could not believe his own eyes. He invited the Americans to come inside and have a glass of wine. They just sat there watching Pan and Laila without saying a word. Suddenly Pan ran across the room to the fireplace, where he had discovered the large red ball on the shelf, Laila got up and gave the ball to him, and Pan started licking and licking it, holding it close.

They were sitting there for hours, talking, and Harold told Laila and her father all they knew about the dog. They were all happy.

"What a story!" Robert exclaimed. "It is too good to be true, and probably no one would believe it."

"Yes, it is quite a tale," Harold said. He was actually a little sad, as he had hoped to take Pan with him to the United States.

They did not leave until late, and Laila and Pan followed their friends to the park gate. Pan was dancing and playing around with his ball. The men all patted Pan good-bye, their hearts beating a little faster. They knew they would never forget Pan. Pan who had saved their lives.

They drove through Oslo's streets thinking this was the only beautiful thing that had happened in the war.

"Dogs never receive any honours; they never become heroes," Robert said, thinking about all the killed dogs he had seen on the front.

They thought about Pan, the dog from the North. They knew he would always be in their hearts. They looked up at the dark sky, soft as velvet, arching overhead with thousands of twinkling stars.

On the steps Laila and Pan sat close to each other. It was a quiet and beautiful night in May 1945. Laila held Pan hard and close, never to lose him again. Pan was trembling, lifting his head towards the sky as a greeting and homage to all his dead friends. His eyes were full of tears, soft, black tears.